AFTER KURUKSHETRA

The Selected Works of Mahasweta Devi

AFTER KURUKSHETRA:

THREE STORIES

MAHASWETA DEVI

Translated by Anjum Katyal

calcutta new delhi 2005

Cover photograph: Naveen Kishore
Cover design: Sunandini Banerjee

ISBN 81 7046 290 8

'Kunti o Nishadi' was first published in *Binodan Bichitra*,
Autumn issue, 1999 and included in *Niranabbui-er Galpo*
(Thema, 2000), 'Panchakanya' appeared in *Proma,* Autumn issue,
2000 and 'Souvali' in *Binodan Bichitra*, Autumn issue, 2000.

*Published by Naveen Kishore, Seagull Books Private Limited
26 Circus Avenue, Calcutta 700 017, India*

*Printed in India by Rockwel Offset
55B Mirza Ghalib Street, Calcutta 700 016*

Contents

the five women

The dharmayuddha is over, the battlefield ablaze with raging
funeral pyres. The dead heroes of the Kauravas and
Pandavas are being cremated with all prescribed ritual detail. As the
pyres burn, a crowd of keening women huddled in the distance cries
out in grief. The only words one can hear amid the wails of mourning are 'Hai! Hai!'

These women are not of the rajavritta, women of royalty, nor are
they servants or attendants. These women are from the families of
the hundreds of foot soldiers—padatiks—from various other little
kingdoms. They had been slaughtered every day, in their thousands,
their function being to protect the chariot-mounted heroes. They
were issued no armour. So they died in large numbers.

As the warriors are cremated, the skies above Kurukshetra are dark with circling birds of prey. Reek of rotting flesh. Row upon row of oil-soaked wood pyres piled high with decomposing bodies. They are set alight. The pyres burn for days.

The pyres burn on and on. The women retreat until they melt into darkness. The prostitute quarters, an essential part of war, now lie abandoned. Did the women shelter in those tents or did they just disappear? No one knows.

The chandals, designated to tend the pyres, to ensure that flesh and bone powder into ash, listen in fear to the eerie wailing that resounds across the horizon, that flows like a swollen river of grief, waves of sorrow swelling and fading in the night. Like a tide, receding into the darkness.

The chandals have no role in war. They arrive when the battle is over. For the past few weeks they have been gathering wood. They knew lots of firewood would be needed. And they knew that they were the ones who would have to finally quench the countless fires of the nameless dead with water. But this was a task they did not fulfill.

—Let the river flood, drown the fires, they said before fleeing.

What had seemed so long a solid wall of darkness now shattered into pieces. The women rose, and began to move.

They were walking back to the outskirts of the capital city. Sunrise saw a procession of black-clad women moving across the landscape. The earth of Kurukshetra was scorched rock hard by the funeral fires. Waves of angry heat. A heat that hung like a haze over the vast cremation ground.

On the outskirts the five women squatted, huddled together. Strips of black cloth covered their breasts, knotted behind. Plain black cloth around their waists, covering their heads.

The head dasi of the royal women's quarters, Madraja, was out looking for recruits. The inner quarters were teeming with countless young widows. Their lives would now be stripped of luxury, of leisure. All those fragrant wreaths of flowers, all that sandal paste and kumkum for the skin, the elaborate oiled and perfumed coiffures, all that—banished from their lives forever.

The acharyas are busy instructing them in the rigorous rules of widowhood. Stunned with grief, the young women silently do as they are told.

Madraja herself was a woman of the Kurujangal region. She saw at a glance that the five women came from the same area. She said, You girls are still young.

The women were silent.

—Going back?

—The earth can bear anything, they say—but that's a lie, you know. It's spewing heat. Hard as rock.

—After what happened . . .

—It's a long, hard way home. Twenty days now . . . Can't take it any more.

Madraja was appraising their legs, shoulders, arms. They were young, it's true. But with bodies used to hard work.

—Arya Subhadra, Venerable Queen, needs women for her widowed daughter-in-law, young Uttara.

—Dasis? Servants?

—She's senseless with grief, struck dumb. And she's also pregnant.

—So?

—During such a disaster . . .

—Disaster? What disaster? Huh, old woman? Was this some natural calamity? So many great kings join in a war between brothers. Some choose one side, some cross over to the other. It wasn't just brother slaughtering brother. We know of quarrels–jealousies–rivalries too. But such a war for just a throne? This, a holy war?! A righteous war?! Just call it a war of greed!'

—All right, I accept that. Now come with me.

—We refuse to serve as dasis, to live as dasis.

—No, no, you'll be Uttara's companions.

This was the understanding on which the five women came to Uttara. In deep sorrow Subhadra said, She shrinks away from familiar faces. Stricken dumb with grief. You have come from the lokavritta outside, from the world of the common man. Stay with her, keep her company.

—What are our duties?

—Nothing in particular. Just do whatever she wants. Ah, my poor child. Like a lotus in full bloom she was. And now! Withering away in the cruel heat of grief.

Uttara sits unmoving, silent. Frowning slightly, she gazes out at the sky.

—Sorrow has turned her into stone.

—Yes, Arya, we can see that.

—You girls are from Kurujangal?

—Girls, wives, yes, from Kurujangal.

The other senior queens entered. Draupadi asks, 'Your names?'

—I'm Godhumi. This is Gomati, holding my hand. That's Yamuna, with the red spot between her brows. That one standing there with a finger on her chin is Vitasta. And this is Vipasha, Vitasta's little sister.

Suddenly Uttara speaks. Named after rivers. How lovely! Arya! Who are they?

Draupadi says with great tenderness, Your companions, dear. They will stay with you. Do whatever you ask them to.

And thus the five women enter Uttara's quarters in the women's wing of the palace.

In time, they become inseparable. Chatting and talking to them, Uttara grows easy and free. For so many days now, she has been frozen in time, speechless and still. A mere slip of a girl, that too pregnant, she has not been able to accept the loss of Abhimanyu.

How anxious her mothers-in-law are! Draupadi, Subhadra, all the others, are deeply worried. If Uttara bears a son, he will be King. It is imperative to keep Uttara in good spirits. How can this be done? She is neither a baby nor a little girl. For however brief a while, she has experienced the love of a man.

They are reassured when they meet the five women. They feel less worried, somehow. When Kunti hears the news she says, Good. They are from a totally different world. Uttara's heart is bound to be lighter in their company.

And with time, that's what happens. Uttara cannot spend a moment without them. She bathes only after they fetch river water for her bath. The mothers-in-law say, A healthy custom. Good for the growing baby in the womb. So many different kinds of advice. The expecting mother is supposed to listen and obey.

Godhumi rests a finger on her cheek and wonders aloud, So many mothers-in-law! How d'you keep count?

—Amongst your people?

—One mother-in-law apiece. Of course, if a man marries more than once, that's a different matter. Then his son's wife has two mothers-in-law.

—Yes, so many mothers-in-law. And then there are the Kaurava widows. You have to include them—

—They're mothers-in-law too?

—Of course!

—Forget it! It's too much! Try and solve this riddle:

No legs and yet it takes flight
No ears but it can hear all right
No eyes but still it has sight!

—Can you guess what it is?

—No, I can't.

The women laugh and tell her, The human mind. It can go anywhere, can hear and understand anything. And even when you shut your eyes, your mind can see everything clearly!

—How true! How true! Uttara claps her hands and laughs in delight, like a child.

Yamuna observes tenderly, O Royal Daughter-in-law! You're really just a little girl!

—Tell me another! Please?

Gomati gestures and says, All right, listen:

First it is born in water

Then it is born on land.

—Wait, wait, let me guess!

—A pearl, silly, a pearl. First it's born inside an oyster, in the water. Then it's taken out when the oyster is pried open, this time on land.

The sound of Uttara's laughter brings Subhadra such relief! Madraja is the one who brought them so it is Madraja whom she now rewards—a diamond-studded bracelet. Madraja says, That Godhumi is a sharp one. They all listen to her.

—So let them! I'll shower them with jewellery! Give them whatever they ask for!

They ask for coloured yarn. Fetching grass and vines, their skilful fingers weave baskets, mats and ropes while they sit and talk.

Their skin is the colour of ripe wheat, their eyes bluish, their coppery hair tightly braided. They dress only in black. All five of them. Indoors, they don't cover their heads. When they go to fetch water, they throw a black cloth over their hair. They fetch water in pitchers of brass burnished like shining gold. They massage Uttara's skin with scented herbal oils. Their touch relaxes her. After a bath, she lounges on a low bed.

This is the time of day when Subhadra comes to keep her daughter-in-law company. The women go off to have their meal. Then they sit in the garden of the women's quarters. Emerald green grass, scattered mango trees entwined with flowering madhavi creepers. The women spread out their wet clothes in the sun. They dry their hair, sit together and talk.

Uttara says, sadly, They don't talk to me like that.

—No matter how fond they are of you, with you they can never be totally free.

—I suppose so.

Today the women sit in a circle, running their fingers through their washed hair, gazing at the sky and humming a tune.

Uttara keeps looking at them. Stray thoughts drift like clouds through her mind. At the moment, Yudhisthira is King. Victory over the Kauravas was total, brutal. The Kaurava women are still reeling from its devastation.

Like a penitent, Kunti nurses Gandhari and Yudhisthira with hands that beg forgiveness as they serve. She observes her sons' arrogance in victory with the distant gaze of a self-exiled onlooker.

The Kauravas are wiped out. Their widowed brides clad in white like silent shadows go about the daily rituals required of them. Endless fasts, pujas, offerings of cows to the brahmans! Their lives rendered empty at such a young age. The life that now lies before them, an unending desert. Each step across that expanse scorched with sorrow.

After Yudhisthira became King, Draupadi would carry on bitterly about the cunning, cruelty and bestiality of the Kauravas.

One day Kunti told her in a low voice, Panchali. Be quiet now. You have borne endless injustice and humiliation. It was to avenge that humiliation that the entire Kaurava clan has been destroyed. But place your hand upon your heart and tell me—have you not been avenged in full? The Kaurava men are all dead. Have you ever looked at the bereft Kaurava women, who have lost their husbands and sons? Are they responsible, tell me?

Draupadi had been silent.

—Try to feel a little compassion, a little pity. A little affection for them. You'll see how it will soften your heart.

No, that was going too far for Draupadi. But she talks less now, is more silent. Keeps herself cloaked in a veil of silence.

Subhadra can't hold back her tears. Slapping her forehead she laments, The sons are dead, their fathers are alive. Daughters-in-law have lost their husbands, while their mothers-in-law are still married.

Gandhari's words come to mind. She had held Krishna Vasudeva responsible for this fratricidal war. She whispers, Arya Gandhari was right. The Yadav clan will perish for the sin of causing this savage war.

She says, Nothing will restore the glories of the past. From now on, history will be nothing but death and destruction.

She spends as much time as she can with Uttara. Abhimanyu is dead. Subhadra still has the company of her husband. And Uttara is carrying Abhimanyu's child.

She thinks, It would be nice if it were a girl. If it's a boy, he too will go to war.

But the experienced, elderly royal midwife says, By the look of her, you'll get a grandson. If I'm right, I expect a plot of good, fertile land. I want to spend the last years of my life in the midst of my children and their families.

Uttara can't sleep. She sits staring out of the window.

—What are you looking at, dear?

—Godhumi and the others. How different they are, Arya!

—How can subject and ruler be the same?

—Five of them, but they're always together. They sleep, wake, eat, bathe, do everything together. They insist on taking me to the garden at daybreak, tell me to walk barefoot on the grass. They make me fold clothes, water the tulsi plant. Do you know why?

—Why, my dear?

—Amongst them, pregnant women don't just lie down and rest. They keep busy doing light chores. They say that it's a law of nature for women to bear children. Just because a woman is pregnant doesn't mean she should indulge and pamper her body. If I keep active, the birth'll be easier for me.

—That's what my midwife used to say as well.

—How they talk, the five of them!

—My child, their life is so different, their language is so different. They must feel good being able to talk in their own tongue.

—What is that song they're singing? I'm trying to follow it, but all I can make out is hai, hai!

—They're not singing, little one. They're lamenting. Can you make out what they're saying?

—Do you know their language?

—Our dasis have always come from that region. I know a little of their tongue. That's a lament.

—But they're singing . . . ?

—A lament for the dead can also be sung. Can you make out the words?

—No, Arya.

—Their husbands were killed in the war too.

—Oh no!

—They are farmers. They grow golden wheat, good quality jowar. Oilseed, spinach, ginger, turmeric, sugarcane, so much more.

Subhadra recalls, They don't need to buy food. The soil of Kurujangal is so rich.

—Yes, so they say.

—When they are sent for, their men go to war, fight, then

return home. This time, no one came back. That's why they're singing a song of mourning:

> The fields of golden wheat lie unploughed, hai hai!
> Who will go there with ox and plough, hai hai!
> Seeds of wheat and sesame lie waiting in store, hai hai!
> They want to be sown
> They want to sprout green leaves
> Bear rich harvest, hai hai!
> Who cast a shroud over the village, hai hai!
> The huts are dark, no lamps are lit
> See the grief in the children's eyes
> In the eyes of the mothers, in the eyes of the wives
> This war's turned villages into cremation grounds, hai hai!

Uttara stares at her in confusion.

—But Arya! All those who gave their lives in the holy war are destined to go to divyalok, to heaven. Were their husbands left behind?

—Who knows? I really can't say.

—How strange! Why did they come here?

Subhadra answers distractedly, Perhaps they were newly weds? Perhaps they were following the battle from a distance? Perhaps they were searching for their husbands' bodies? Did the rajavritta—the royalty—ever care to know about the janavritta—common humanity?

—Their husbands . . . never . . . went to heaven?

—I don't know, dear. Don't trouble your mind with such thoughts. In your condition . . .

—Arya, is what they say true?

—What do they say?

—They say the pyres blazed for many days. That the earth was burning hot and baked rock hard.

—It could be.

—They have to take the long route to the river. The straight
road burns their feet.

Subhadra is dry-eyed and trembling. With deep tenderness she
says, Go to sleep, dear. Rest awhile.

Earlier, Uttara could not sleep. If the lamps weren't kept burning, she would wake with a start. Her dreams were full of
Abhimanyu's bloodied body and she, wiping away tirelessly at his
wounds with the edge of her saree.

Now, she sleeps through the night. The five women sleep beside
her on the floor, on blankets. Godhumi's hand never leaves her side.
Their husbands are dead too. Yet they sleep.

As she falls asleep Uttara murmurs, How pretty your names
are . . .'

Named after rivers, named after food grains. Will Uttara have a
boy or a girl? What will the child's name be?

—What will you call your child?

—That's not up to me.

—Then who'll decide?

—Oh, it's an elaborate process! Pujas, yagnas, offerings to Agni,
the elder males of the family will sit together to discuss it, the priests
will study the signs, the acharya will draw up the horoscope. It's they
who'll choose a name for the child.

—Goodness! Your ways are so-o different!

—These are the rituals. Don't you have them too?

—Of course we do. The baby is weighed against food grains.
One of the grandparents chooses a name. Its head is shaved. Then
it's bathed in water warmed by the sun. Musicians play and the
women sing. Then its maternal uncle feeds it a bit of ghee-payesh
with the little finger of his right hand.

—And then?

—The baby feeds and falls asleep. The villagers are treated to a
feast. We all sing and have a good time.

—Even the women?

—Of course! The women, the men, the old people! Why do you think I was named Godhumi? My skin was the colour of ripe wheat, so my grandmother said, Let's call her Godhumi.

—Really, I know nothing about anything! Imagine men and women, singing together . . .

Gomati looks away and speaks to herself, Who bothers to find out what our villages are like? As the wheat begins to ripen, the birds arrive. All day long the boys and girls shout, make a noise, keep the birds at bay. We make huge scarecrows of straw to frighten off the birds.

Vipasha says, The men keep watch over the fields all night long.

—Why?

—Because deer come to eat the crop. So they have to guard the fields.

—I know nothing . . .

—You're really simple, aren't you? If the farmers didn't pay with food grain, the royal granary would be empty.

—A startled deer's such a pretty sight!

Vitasta says, Not just the men, the women also guard the fields. Once my mother speared a deer to death. My mother is really strong. She can lift a stone grinder all by herself.

—But the spear . . . is a man's weapon . . .

Gomati smiles gravely. It's a foot soldier's weapon, Princess. Only peasants make foot soldiers.

Vitasta, busy chiselling wings for a small clay bird said, A woman's weapon too.

Vitasta's fingers are always busy. She fetches clay from the river bank. She makes little clay figures: birds, horses, deer, carts, men, mothers with children. Bakes them in the heat of the sun, paints them. She is making little toys for Uttara's baby.

Gomati says once more, No armour, no bows and arrows. The foot soldier's only weapon is the spear. She keeps her gaze lowered as she speaks. Her gaze is veiled always, as though by a dark curtain. No one can guess at her thoughts. Her eyes, like the dark, immeasurably deep lakes of the Himalayas. Their depths never fathomed by man, the lakes are still and silent. Uttara has heard of these lakes in her childhood, from her nurse.

—Women know how to use the spear?

—Every household has them. When the men go off to war, we women protect our homes.

—But Vitasta's mother speared a deer! So sad!

Godhumi said, What's so sad about it, Princess? The royal kitchens cook venison every day. Deer hide is used to make shoes, rugs . . . So we hunt deer, even birds. Eat their meat.

—I see . . . look, I'm asking silly questions because I don't know anything . . . please don't be angry with me.

Madraja says, Why do you have to be so familiar with them? They're growing insolent. I'm going to tell Arya to get you new dasis.

—No!

—As it is you're with child, on top of that newly widowed, at a time like this . . .

—Get out!

The word 'widow' terrifies her. It scares her, the thought of the white-clad Kaurava widows. She can't recognize herself in the mirror. When was it that she laughed, played, learned dance from Brihannala?[1] Who was she who threw tantrums, demanded fine silk clothes to dress her dolls in?

That Uttara had long unbound tresses hanging loose about her as she danced in the wind. That Uttara loved to spend hours on her swing, played in the garden for hours with her companions. That Uttara dressed in brightly coloured cholis, ghagras and chunnis.

This Uttara wears plain white, no ornaments, her hair hangs heavy on her shoulders. This Uttara's eyes and mouth have forgotten how to smile, her footsteps are timid, hesitant. How long will she have to survive? How long will that strange reflection haunt her in the mirror?

At best, her child will stay with her a year. After that, the wet nurses will take over its upbringing. Royal offspring are not raised by their mothers.

Then will begin the prescribed rites and rituals, the self-denial, the penance.

Just six months of married life. How fleeting her happiness! Such a young groom, such a young bride. What a fuss was made of her when she entered her married home as a bride! Kunti took both bride and groom onto her lap and said, I loved to play with clay dolls as a child. These are my dolls come alive. Uttara was everyone's darling.

She whispers to herself, What a joyous wedding it was.

Everything now, no more than a dream. No more than a fairytale heard as a child.

How festive the marriage mandap had been! How sweet the music! Outside the palace, like a carnival of wandering gypsies. Men and women in brightly coloured clothes, dancing gaily. Vaulting up and down bamboo poles. Someone had a performing bear, others were distributing lac bangles. Like a market of joy.

In the marriage mandap, the fire ceremony was being held. The flames licking at the slivers of wood dipped in ghee, blazing up into the air. The royal women sitting in a row. Uttara couldn't take her eyes off the chief queen of the Pandavas, Draupadi. Her dignity, grace and beauty seemed to put the others to shame.

Had all this really happened in Uttara's life?

On the pond in her garden, swans float by with regal grace. Had Uttara once been as free and as graceful as them, living in her father's house?

A dream, all just a dream! From the roof of her father's house she could see the distant mountain ranges. That country had hills and deserts, forests and streams . . . Caravans of nomadic traders. Their goods packed onto camel back, they would come from places like Gandhara, Kekaya, Taxila, Trigartha. Wandering magicians. Snake charmers. Dancers and puppeteers roamed the streets. Told wondrous tales and sang as they made their puppets dance.

Those happy times now seem no more than a dream.

Suddenly she feels angry.

She orders Madraja, They are to stay.

Madraja has been chief dasi in the royal inner quarters for a long time. She is used to being in control. Used to telling the Pandava queens what to do.

—They make you restless.

—No they don't. It's this silent palace of mourning . . .

—What mourning, oh Widow of Abhimanyu! All those who lost their lives to the righteous war have gone straight to divyalok! What a hubbub of joy in heaven! Just think . . .

Godhumi says, Oh yes! Seen the chariots from heaven with your own eyes, haven't you? Heard the joyful ululation with your own ears?

—How can that be!

—At least the chariot then? Descending from heaven . . .?

—Go on with you! I was inside at the time . . .

—Then why say all this?

—Everyone knows it's true.

—Shame on you, Madraja! A woman from Kurujangal! Yet talk like the rajavritta?

—They brought me here when I was just a babe. Nothing new about that. We're the ones they always get. Dasis for the royal household, courtesans for the palace, prostitutes for the soldiers. Just like you girls.

—No. We weren't brought here like you. We never imagined we would end up in the rajavritta. We were married into farming families. Our husbands were sent for during the war. We knew the foot soldiers would die in huge numbers. We'd watch the fighting from afar. At the close of each day's battle we'd search for our husbands' bodies in the heart of that awful darkness. Little clay lamps in our hands, or flaming torches of deodar wood. Our husbands, our brothers, our brothers-in-law . . . and—hear this, Madraja!

Godhumi says, No chariots came down from divyalok. They did not go to heaven. The foot soldiers died fighting in the very same dharmayuddha. But no funeral rites were held for their souls.

—The five of you came here.

—We could not go home.

Uttara can hear a savage undertone to Godhumi's words. Abhimanyu had once told her, Under the surface of a flowing river lurks another current, a strong undertow which is primeval, savage. Or else how could a river sweep an elephant off its feet?

She suddenly enquires in genuine concern, Why, Godhumi? Why couldn't you go back?

Godhumi replies, Princess! What was left, to go back to? Foot soldiers come from Ahichhatra, Matsya, Kurujangal, Kosala, Trigartha, Dwaitava, Panchal, Prachya. We are from Kurujangal. Hai! We don't know about other places. But our fields, our rich fields, watered all year long by rivers, are lying bereft of crops. Day after day, the war heroes massacred hordes of foot soldiers. Our men died in droves.

Vitasta appears to take up the second stanza of the song, The lamps lie unlit in village homes . . . we untethered the cattle before coming away . . . they must have fallen prey to wild beasts by now . . .

Vipasha says, No one grinds the grains of wheat into flour in the village huts, no women churn milk to make butter, no one extracts oil from oilseeds, all the sounds of a village lie silenced . . .

Yamuna says, Along the river bank no women wash and launder clothes. Mothers don't bathe and massage their babies . . .

Gomati's voice, harsh with grief, says, Married women no longer sing as they walk to the river to collect water with which to bathe a new bride . . .

The five women speak as one, Where would we have gone?

Uttara stares at them. She says, Stay with me.

Godhumi shakes her head sadly. Says, These are chambers of silence.

—Silence?

—Everything happens outside the women's quarters, here. Pujas, ceremonial sacrifices, yagnas. There, the world is full of bustle and activity. Here, you white-clad widows float around like shadowy ghosts. We wonder, won't you ever laugh, talk loudly, run outside on restless feet?

—No!

Subhadra comes in, joins them. Rajavritta widows must follow the example set by Arya Kunti. In ihalok, in this world of ours, widows have no right to happiness. You women may leave.

Uttara surprises even herself when she cries out, No, Arya! With them around . . . I feel . . .

She bursts into tears. I feel as if I'm alive!

Subhadra holds her close, strokes her head gently and calms her down.

—Madraja shouldn't order me around!

—She won't. Shush, now, dear. You have a baby in your womb . . .

—This silence suffocates me!

—Calm down, dear.

Uttara sobs heartbrokenly and then gradually grows calmer. Subhadra's mind is in turmoil. Who can she consult? And what will she ask?

Deeply distressed, she begs, Girls!

—Yes, Arya?

—Please don't let her get agitated. Her baby . . . will suffer . . .

This Subhadra was not the favoured sister of Krishna Vasudeva speaking. This was a concerned mother like any other.

—We'll be leaving soon, Arya. We would have left already. But it's still impossible to cross the battlefield of Kurukshetra. So many pyres burned for so many days, that the ground is baked rock hard, searing hot. Our feet get burnt. How can we walk so far over that scorched earth?

Madraja says, The others like them are still living on the outskirts.

—Just don't upset my daughter-in-law.

Subhadra's heart, like that of any woman, feels close to bursting with those words. The five women exchange glances. Shake their heads, sigh, and turn away.

Subhadra says, I'll stay with her.

The five women seem to think as one. They are so close that they seem to understand each other without words, speak to one another with their eyes alone. They look, they understand.

They ask Uttara, Are you better now?

—Yes.

—Look how lovely these mother-and-child clay dolls are. Vitasta's made them.

Vitasta says, If I knew where the potters' colony was, I'd have had them fired in kilns. The colours look even prettier on red, baked clay.

—Did you make these dolls at home as well?

—Yes, and I gave them to children to play with.

—They must have been so happy!

Uttara's eyes, as innocent as a child's. Vitasta says, Your baby will be happy too, playing with them.

—And all of you . . . don't you . . .

The five women shake their heads. A strange tale. They were all married on the same day. They had just arrived at their new homes when the horns had sounded, summoning the young men to war. The preparations for war had begun.

Yamuna is a quiet sort, a woman of few words. She says, The men go first. Then we have to carry on.

—If you were in the village, what would you be doing?

—Cleaning the hut and the yard, collecting firewood, fetching water from the river.

—I don't know that life.

—How could you be expected to, Princess?

—Did you sing as you worked?

—Yes, dear.

—I've never seen a village. But troupes of wandering singers, puppeteers, dancers would come often, and I loved to listen to their songs . . . watch their dances . . . before I was married.

The women exchange glances. They ask, What stories did your dhatri, your nurse, tell you at the time? Can you remember?

—Not always. Sometimes I remember . . . when you talk of your life . . . it all sounds so unfamiliar . . . I know so little . . .

—Do you want to hear about our people?

—What do they do?

The women throw up their hands in wonder at her question. What else! They tell tales and sing songs as they do their chores.

Such amazing fairytales! It seems their mothers-in-law too churn milk, turn it into butter, curds and ghee.

They comb, oil and braid the hair of their daughters and daughters-in-law. And tell stories to their grandchildren.

—Don't you visit the town?

—No, dear. The town doesn't know us, and we don't know the town. And now . . . no one will come here anymore.

—Why?

—Such a savage war, so much destruction, who will come to the town after this? Tell us, such a terrible war and all in the family—isn't it a terrible sin?

—But it was a dharmayuddha, a righteous war.

—Dharmayuddha!

Godhumi speaks in deep compassion, So many hundreds of widows! So many homes in which mothers have lost their sons!

—Yes . . . old Arya Gandhari lost a hundred sons . . . my mothers-in-law lost their . . .

Suddenly Godhumi says, Listen! Listen, isn't that the chatak calling?

They listen intently. Uttara can hear a bird call, who knows what bird? Far in the distance, fading away.

—It's a chatak all right!

—What happens when a chatak calls?

Godhumi seems to have drifted away, far away, somewhere near that unseen bird. She says, dreamily, The chatak only drinks rain-water . . . It must have sighted rain clouds, that's why it's calling.

—And then?

—It will rain.

—And after it rains?

—The earth will be quenched.

Kurukshetra will grow cool. The waves of heat will die down. And perhaps, just perhaps, some day grass will grow green there again.

And the rains come, with a great roar of sound, pouring down with furious urgency. The trees in the garden of the women's quarters are bathed by the showers. Madraja says, The wise ones have said that it's bound to rain after a war like this.

After a few days of steady rain, after satiating the parched earth, the clouds move off with slow majesty towards the east.

Yamuna whispers, Wherever they find forest, they will give rain.

Madraja says, Look at the clouds swollen with rain! Heading east, towards the land of Arya Chitrangada.[2] A sure sign of the monsoon.

Once the rains pass over, the five women present themselves to Uttara and say, The earth has grown cool, now, Princess. Time for us to leave.

—What do you mean?

Madraja runs to fetch Arya Subhadra. She in turn sends for Arya Draupadi. The news races through the inner quarters. One by one the queens arrive. Uttara clutches at the edge of Subhadra's saree.

—They're going away!

—You're going away?

—Yes, Arya. The earth is cool now. We can walk across it, now.

Uttara asks, Why do you have to go?

Godhumi says, We have to get married.

—Get married?! But you're . . .

—Our husbands were foot soldiers. We looked and looked for their bodies every evening after battle. Finally, Mahatma Vidura[3] . . . after eighteen days . . . arranged a mass cremation for all the foot soldiers . . . so many pyres burning . . . the earth was baked rock hard, fire-hot . . .

—That's why you came here, isn't it?

—We couldn't walk across that burning earth. The outskirts

were full of women like us. We were looking for familiar faces . . . and Madraja brought us here.

—Why are you leaving?

The five women folded their hands. When we are widowed, we marry our brothers-in-law. That is the custom in our janavritta community.

—Are there any young men left?

—We don't know. But now that it has rained, the fields are lying unploughed, the villages untended. We must go.

—You foolish girls! Who will marry you?

—We don't know, Arya Subhadra. But someone or the other will. Arya! We worship the earth. After a terrible calamity, the sun always rises. Even after this dreadful war, Nature has not stood still.

Draupadi draws a deep breath. In the silence of that room, the sound is clearly heard. All eyes are turned on the five women in astonishment.

Who has ever really looked at them? Nothing more than insignificant presences. But now, suddenly, those presences have been granted form, granted notice.

Thick dark hair, neatly combed, caught back and braided, black cloth across their breasts, limbs draped in black, strongly muscled necks and shoulders, arms, fingers and legs showing signs of hard work.

—If we don't go . . . the fields will lie fallow, the cattle will be uncared for. Once we return, all of us together will perform the necessary funerary rituals for our dead. Then the elders will arrange marriages. We need husbands, we need children. The village needs to hear the sound of chatter and laughter. We will . . . create life. That's what Nature teaches us.

—But . . .

—Life wants that as well, Arya Subhadra! Respected majesties! As long as there is life, that life demands fulfilment. Our widows remarry, are respected by their families. They work alongside their husbands cultivating the land, harvesting and storing the crop. They never deny the demands of life in order to exist as mere shadowy ghosts, shrouded in silence. Once we had husbands, now we don't. Crying won't bring them back to life. Also, our husbands fought and died in the king's war. No divyalok for them. That's only for the rajavritta.

—All those who give their lives to the dharmayuddha will attain heaven, girls.

—This was not our dharmayuddha. Brother kills brother, uncle kills nephew, shishya kills guru. It may be your idea of dharma, it's not ours.

Vitasta places a woven grass basket full of clay toys at Uttara's feet. Says, Don't cry, dear. Your baby will play with these. And some day, while going somewhere, if you ever see birds wheeling over fields ripe with grain, smoke rising from village kitchen fires, or hear a chorus of voices raised in song, just think to yourself—that must be their homeland.

They bow before the queens. Now the senior queen, Draupadi, comes forward. Touching their heads in blessing she says, Go, go towards your fulfilment.

Then she asks, Will you come to see Uttara's child?

—Yes, we will. And we'll sit here in the garden and sing songs to the baby.

They turn to leave. Draupadi speaks in a choked voice, May you find peace, may you find fulfilment, may you return to the world of the everyday life.

The five women walk out. Godhumi turns back and says, The water for your bath's ready, my dear.

Uttara picks up the basket of dolls.

And thinks to herself, May you all be happy.

Notes

1 Brihannala: Arjuna had, during his period of training in weaponry in Heaven, rejected Urvashi, the celestial dancer, for which she had cursed him: he would remain sexless for a year. During the one year that the Pandavas spent incognito, Arjuna assumed the disguise of a eunuch named Brihannala trained in the arts of music and dance which he taught to the ladies of the royal household.

2 Arya Chitrangada: One of Arjuna's wives, daughter of Chitrabhanu, King of Manipur.

3 Vidura: Born to Ambika's sudra handmaiden, fathered by Vyasa (the author of the Mahabharata). Sagacious and wise, he was a father-figure to the Pandavas, advising them on every decision.

kunti and the nishadin

It is Kunti who has to tend to Dhritarashtra and Gandhari in this the final chapter of their life, the retreat into the forest. Kunti feels that it is, after all, her duty to look after the elderly brother-in-law and his wife who-chooses-not-to-see-with-her-eyes. This is a forest ashram, not a royal palace. She is the one who collects the firewood for the daily ceremonies of fire.

The afternoons are a magical time. She leaves the ashram and goes into the forest. She takes a rope woven from grass, binds the wood into a bundle, rests a while, then drags the firewood back to the ashram. Had Bhima been around he would never have let her do this chore.

One day she sees some middle-aged nishadins[1] moving about the forest with their children and families. Are they indeed middle-aged? The occasional silver strand of hair would suggest so. Such strong limbs, muscled shoulders! They gather wood. Tie it in bundles bound with forest vines. At sundown they heft these bundles onto their heads. Then they spark flint, light flaming torches of wood and follow the jungle path home. Singing their own songs. Kunti has never tried to learn the language they speak.

This forest is full of tall, resinous trees. They gather this resin, honey, tubers and roots. They seem to be a tranquil, happy, hard-working lot, their faces always wreathed in bright smiles.

Resin trickles down the tree trunks. The incense-scented breeze soothes Kunti's weary, wasted body and relieves her fatigue. Watching the nishadins, it strikes her for the first time that she is wasting herself living like this, subsisting on rotting, withered leaves. Blindly following a predetermined predestined path to death.

Kunti can now look back. She never knew that she carried within her such a burden of unspoken thoughts and feelings. Life in the rajavritta was so different. Mother of the Pandavas. Wife of Pandu. The role of daughter-in-law, the role of queen, the role of mother, playing these hundreds of roles where was the space, the time to be her true self? All that while—amazingly—she never felt that anything was hers, hers alone.

Once, just once, in the first fragrant bloom of youth . . . the memory burns inside her like a funeral pyre. It will rage unabated till she dies.

Now, she can't bear to keep it all locked inside her. If only she could unburden herself to this forest, these rocks, birds, insects, withered leaves! The nishad women move around, sometimes close, sometimes at a distance. But there is no exchange of words with them. Her body worn thin by observing numerous religious austerities, white haired, clad in a length of white silk cloth of unblemished purity, Kunti's eyes are the only thing about her still alive. Yet those eyes register nothing about the nishadins moving about in front of her, not even by a look.

How could they? Her life had been the rajavritta, the gods, serving the brahmans. Had she ever spoken to a dasi? Had she developed any genuine bond with Hidimba?[2] Life outside the rajavritta had not touched her at all.

Why are these nishadins moving about so close to her? She doesn't care. Kunti just wants to lay bare her deepest thoughts, lying heavy in her heart. She needs to confess.

Gandhari and her bandaged eyes fill Kunti with awe. How stately she is! The loss of a hundred sons has not succeeded in shattering her composure. Gandhari knows that she has always walked the right path, is still doing her duty, will do so till her dying day.

But Kunti needs to speak. She still has something to say. Every day she feels weaker, more exhausted. Looking after Dhritarashtra and Gandhari, settling them safely in the ashram hut, she feels as if she can hardly move—when will she be able to speak her mind? She may as well talk to these trees, the river, the birds, the murmuring leaves, the wind, even to the nishadins. Who, even if they hear her, won't understand. Won't ask any questions. When the sun sets in the west, they will leave, and Kunti will return to the ashram. Arrange for Dhritarashtra and Gandhari's evening rituals. Sup off pulped leaves. Drink some water, and lie down to sleep on the grass mat.

Was there a time when she slept on a sandalwood bed, on sheets as soft and white as the froth on milk? When she feasted on seven kinds of dishes, rice soaked in ghee, ate off golden platters? Was it she who made all the arrangements for the many yagnas, kept fasts during the pujas?

Which Kunti was it who called upon the Sun, who was herself as beautiful as the rising sun's crimson rays . . . whose cloud of dense black hair the dasis dried with fragrant incense smoke . . . who would go to her husband elaborately dressed and adorned with jewellery? Yudhisthira, Bhima and Arjuna were born of her womb, but they were not sired by Pandu.[3] Did she lavish love on Nakula and Sahadeva because they were motherless boys?[4] Or was she just playing the role expected of her? Where was her courage? Her dharma? Kunti talks to herself. How is she to be purged and cleansed if she does not first confess?

O Mother Earth, protector of the forests–hills–waters and all living things, hear what Kunti has to say!

I am not truly pious and dutiful like Gandhari. I lack the courage that comes from dharma. I was overwhelmed to find my sons alive after the battle of Kurukshetra. But Draupadi and Uttara were devastated at the death of their sons. I could not console them. Gandhari did.

I saw how, even after the loss of a hundred sons, she consoled them. She told them over and over again, this massacre was pre-ordained, unavoidable. Like you, I too have lost my sons. Who will console whom? This chapter of death is now past. Come, let us dry our tears. We must not allow ourselves to be undone by grief. Harden your hearts. Of course death is nothing but an epic of sorrow. But we wives, mothers, daughters and sisters have to live on. To survive we need courage and the strength to bear pain. Because this grief is going to be our lifelong companion.

No, I have none of Gandhari's true piety and righteousness. When, before Krishna, she mourned the dead, was it only her dead sons and grandsons, the countless widows, she lamented over? As she sat with the dead Abhimanyu's body in her lap, every time she raised her voice to cry aloud I realized. She was cursing war and bloodshed on behalf of all the women in this world.

That's what makes her Gandhari. This war was a battle for power. A war to wipe out the other and establish oneself as all-powerful. Did dharma triumph? Was adharma vanquished? The heartrending wails of the women at the sight of all those bloodied, savaged corpses was a curse on the word 'war' itself!

And O Mother Earth, listen to me!

Brighter than a flame he was . . . uncompromising, archer of archers . . . Karna looked so much at peace as he lay there, dead. Gandhari's piercing cry at the sight of Karna's body struck me like a whip.

Why did I not have the courage? To cradle Karna's severed head in my lap and say, This is my firstborn? Dhananjaya!⁵ You have murdered your eldest brother! The son I abandoned for fear of public shame! Had I not disowned him, my name would have been sullied forever.

Karna is the only one of my sons whose father I took of my own free will.

What irony! What irony! Not one of the five Pandavas is sired by Pandu! Yet they are Pandavas. And Karna? A carpenter's son.

O Ancient Mother! That day Kunti stayed silent. What greater sin can there be?

Gandhari knew she was pure and innocent. This knowledge gave her the courage to publicly speak the truth.

Else would she have been able to curse Krishna? That Krishna who could have stopped the war but instead was the cause of it?

Fearless. Upright. Unshakeable and sure of herself, Gandhari cursed Krishna.

And I, silent, listened.

I don't deserve your forgiveness. The wealth and power of the royal palace, the might of the son who ruled on the throne, all that tore me apart.

Thus this lonely forest, this closeness to nature, the daily sunsets—all this shows me how petty and ignoble human beings are.

Where? Where is the effect, here, in nature's kingdom, of that massive and meaningless battle for power, that senseless bloodbath, that massacre? Where?

Earlier, my eyes could not see, my mind could not understand.

But I have lashed my conscience over and over. And I have realized. If I do not speak out now, it will be the ultimate sin.

Suddenly Kunti lifted her head. Stone-faced, unmoving, the nishadins were staring at her.

Kunti was speechless.

The elderly nishadin said something to the others, who knows what. They fell over each other laughing.

Kunti was trembling, terrified. Would they come closer?

Their shadows may fall on the firewood for the sacred rites and defile it.

Evening was approaching. Kunti stood up. Her thin fingers tightened on the grass rope as she dragged the bundle away. She would find another spot tomorrow. After today's confession, it felt as if she was finding herself again. As if she was being cleansed. Amazing, how light she felt. Worry doesn't just burn your soul but is a heavy burden as well.

Talking before the nishadins was the same as talking to the rocks and stones. To the earth.

They did not know her language, and she did not know theirs.

When Kunti helped her lie down, Gandhari said to her, O Mother of the Five Pandavas! The touch of your hands is always cool. But today they feel warmer. As if the blood is circulating through your veins. Even your touch is alive, today.

—The forest feels as warm as a mother's embrace, O Elder One!

—Do you find peace?

—Perhaps.

—Free your mind from earthly cares.

—I don't have your strength of character. But I try.

—With every passing second we move towards the end. I am waiting for death.

—Yes, O Elder One.

Kunti lay down on the grass mat at their feet. No one had wanted her to come away. It was all right for Dhritarashtra and Gandhari
to leave for the forest ashram. But why should the mother of the
Emperor of Jambudwipa, girdled by the seven seas, go with them?

Kunti said to herself, Life in the rajavritta was tearing me apart.

Today, for no reason at all, Kunti bathed in the forest stream again.
Her white hair left loose, she sat with her back turned to the sun.
What if the Sun looked down at her today? Would He even recognize her? A million years for mankind are a mere instant for the
gods.

Why does she feel this urge to confess everything? No, she does-
n't think the nishadins come to this part of the forest. The trees and
bushes look the same, it is possible to confuse one's way. But
Vidura[6] had taught her well. As you move through the forest, break
a branch, place a stone under a tree, carve a sign, and you won't lose
your way.

He had said, Aranyaka, the spirit of the forest, herself shies away
from human beings. She knows the forest tribes well. They never
lose their way. But Aranyaka's magic leads outsiders astray. Keep the
kingshuk tree on the path to the ashram in mind. And don't stray
too far.

—Is there anything to be afraid of?

—Fear is a state of mind.

The forest feels good. No wide roads, no rows of shops, no cav-
alry marching up and down, no thundering wheels of royal chariots
rumbling by.

Here, one can be alone with oneself. Here, one can whisper and
confess.

O Devi Vasundhara! O Mother Earth! After Kurukshetra,
countless funeral pyres were lit. All those foot soldiers who were

drafted from faraway lands and who sacrificed their lives in the battle were, at Yudhisthira's orders, burned on mass pyres organized by Vidura. The air was thick with the stench of burning flesh. To cover the stink of putrefaction, ghee and camphor were poured onto the flames. But the fumes of death may not be so easily hid.

I hesitated no more. I haven't committed just one sin, after all. I hadn't told my sons about the birth of Karna. Then, the day before the battle, I went to Karna and told him, Abandon Duryodhana, side with Yudhisthira. And yet he did nothing to insult me.

—I said, Son! You were born of my womb. Do as I tell you.

How intolerable the depths of my audacity! He could have said in reply, Just nurturing a child in your womb is not enough. You sacrifice him after birth, you carry out none of the responsibilities of motherhood—how can you now demand from him obedience as a son?

—But he did not.

—The reason I didn't go to him was that I was driven mad by love. I didn't worry about him at all, didn't think of him even once. All my concern was for the Pandavas.

But Gandhari raised her voice high in lamentation over Karna. She cried aloud, For thirteen years, Yudhisthira couldn't sleep for fear of Karna. Karna was as unvanquishable as Indra, as brave as Agni, as serene as Himalaya. May I be cursed, I stood there, silent.

Living in the rajavritta makes one cunning, treacherous. I never visited Karna hungering to hold him to my bosom. For my sons' sake, I told him to leave Duryodhana, join Yudhisthira. Now I feel, Karna knew that the clever trickster Vasudev Krishna would ensure that victory went to the Pandavas. Only the wars of the victorious are known as dharmayuddha. The wars of the vanquished are never called thus. Knowing this . . . Karna said . . . he could not abandon Duryodhana. Apart from Arjuna, he would not harm any of the other Pandavas—You will still have five sons left alive.

Which means he considered himself one of my sons. And I . . .

I never once said to him, The memory of abandoning you at birth tortures me daily, burns me up inside. Why didn't I? Because I didn't suffer over his loss. I felt no yearning for him. The Pandavas were my primary concern. So I said to him, You say you mean your brothers no harm, then you must look out for them.

—Curse me! Curse the Mother of the Five Pandavas! When the cremations were over, when Karna was nothing but ashes, I told Yudhisthira, When you perform the tarpan, do one for Karna as well. He was fathered by Suryadeva, borne in my womb, my first-born son.

When he asked me why, why, why I had not told him this before, I knew that my sons would always hold this question against me. Because Yudhisthira, after the tarpan ceremony on the banks of the Ganges, asked me, How did it come about that he was sired by a god and born of your womb?

To ask such a question of me! Yudhisthira! You are five brothers yet not one of you was sired by Pandu. I could have answered your question. I could have said, It 'came about' in just the same way that you, Bhima and Arjuna were sired by Dharma, Vayu and Indra and born of my womb. Just as Nakula and Sahadeva were sired by the Ashwinikumaras and born of Madri's womb. Karna was sired by Suryadeva and born of mine.

Yudhisthira! You ask me 'why?'

No, I never even thought of doing anything on my own. Pandu told me, A woman can beget sons with the aid of another man. I got my lord's permission, I went ahead. The only time I took a man I wanted, of my own free will, I got Karna. I was unmarried then, there was no need for a husband's assent. In today's society, Yudhisthira, if her husband should wish it, a woman can beget a child sired by another. But no young girl can become a mother of her own free will. Madhavi, the rishi's daughter, on her father's command, bore four sons sired by four different men. She was unmarried. But she was carrying out her father's orders, so society accepted her.

I am Pandu's wife, my husband is not the father of my sons, yet you are all Pandavas. But Karna will never be any more than a carpenter's son.

I feel that some day, the future will grant Karna the respect and honour he deserves.

But not to me.

Pouring her heart out to Mother Earth, Kunti lifted her head. The elderly nishadin watched her, her chin upon a rock.

And, wonder of wonder, her eyes seem to be speaking to Kunti. A bolt of lightning sears through Kunti's brain. That gaze, full of pity.

Pity? For Kunti? The nishadin was pitying her?

She bent down, tied the small bundle of wood firmly with the rope, and walked away.

At times the ashram seems so close, today it feels far, far away. One sees mirages in a desert. A spot of water, now so close, now so distant. But this was a forest, not a desert.

All at once she saw the flowering kingshuk tree and beside it, the ashram.

Clasping Kunti's hands in her thin, old, ivory-hued fingers, Gandhari whispered, Calm down, calm down, O Mother of the Pandavas! Calm down. Time moves in cycles, circling like the wheels of the chariot. Our life cycle is shrinking. Soon it will be just a dot. And finally even that dot will merge into the void.

—Yes, O Elder One.

—Don't blame yourself too harshly. No matter how hard you try, you can never bring back the past, never turn yesterday into tomorrow. See, today's sunrise was real, so was the sunset. We will fall asleep but time will keep moving. And tomorrow, it will give us yet another sunrise.

Touching Gandhari's feet, Kunti lay down on the grass mat. She prayed silently, Sleep! Come soon! Lay my mind at rest.

This afternoon, as Kunti was about to sit on a rock under a tree in the forest, she felt an unease in the usually peaceful place, as if the breeze itself was spreading a sense of alarm.

She grew alert, watchful.

Today the forest was not quiet. Flocks of birds were leaving their nests and flying away. Monkeys were leaping from tree to tree, vanishing into the depths of the forest. Astonishingly, even herds of cheetal were fleeing somewhere.

What has happened?

Nishad men–women–children with their pet hunting dogs were walking off, carrying bundles of belongings on their heads.

Well, let them go. Let them desert the forest. Today Kunti would ask Mother Earth, where had she gone wrong, what was her crime, when would she be able to forgive herself?

She started at the sight of someone's shadow.

The elderly nishadin.

Kunti raised astonished eyes. Why was this dark-skinned woman carved of black stone standing so close to her? Bending down towards her? Searching her eyes?

—No confessing of sins today?

—You . . . you . . .

—I've heard you out day after day, waiting to see if you will confess your gravest sin.

—Your language . . . like mine . . . ?

—Oh yes, I not only understand it, I speak it too. Of course you never thought of us as human, did you? No more than the mute rocks, or trees, or animals.

—But . . . you never spoke a word . . .

—Today's the day I've been waiting for. We've been seeking you for years. We don't enter the town, you see. In the end you came to us, it was bound to be. We've waited years for you, Kunti!

—You know my name?

The nishadin laughed. She said, It hurts, doesn't it? That a nishadin should call you by name? Yes, I took your name. In this forest you are defenceless, Kunti. Your sons are not with you, they can't send in their soldiers to punish us.

—Do you know that rishis dwell in this forest?

—Oh, we see plenty of rishis about. This is the land of our birth, you know. Devi Aranyaka is our mother.

Abruptly, Kunti felt drained and exhausted. They had come to the forest ashram from Gangadwar. Wishing to do penance and starve her emaciated body to death. Why, then, did she feel offended at a nishadin's effrontery in addressing her by name?

—What is it, nishadin, what do you want?

—You haven't confessed to your greatest sin.

—Yes I have. You follow my language, you heard me.

—No, Kunti! That was a sin committed during your rajavritta life even though your son was not yet King.

—I spoke of Karna too.

—The rajavritta folk and the lokavritta folk have different values, different ideas of right and wrong. If a young nishad girl makes love to the boy of her choice and gets pregnant, we celebrate it with a wedding.

—What kind of law is that?

—Nature's law. Nature abhors waste. We honour life. When a man and woman come together, they create a new life. But you won't understand.

—What are you saying? That my confession has no value?

—For you it does. Not for us. But to the people of the lokavritta, to sacrifice or harm innocents in one's own self-interest is the most unpardonable sin. You are guilty of that sin.

—I? Against the lokavritta?

—Remember the town of Varanavata, Kunti?

—Yes, I went there many many years ago . . .

—Let me jog your memory. You stayed there, in the house of lac, Jatugriha?

—Yes, it was a plot by Duryodhana . . .

—Remember how it was rumoured that you and your five sons had burnt to death there?

—But . . . that was . . .

—A scheme, right? A cruel plot? Only the rajavritta can do such a thing. You live there for one year, knowing full well that the place will be burned to ashes, that you have to save yourself and your sons. You had to provide irrefutable proof that the six of you had been burned to death. Nishads and nishadins were regular visitors there, weren't they?

—But . . .

—Shut up. Listen. They would come from the forest. They supplied timber, animal hides, ivory, venison, medicinal herbs, resin, honey. They, both men and women, would sell their wares in exchange for salt–clothes–rice. Then they would drink some wine, sing and dance arm in arm and return home. Jatugriha was on the edge of town. It lay on their path home.

—Yes.

—Tell me, who knew of a certain elderly nishadin and her five young sons? Who invited them to her feast for brahmans? Who made sure that they were served with unlimited amounts of wine? You have held feasts for so many brahmans so many times, Kunti. How often have you invited any nishad–kirat–sabar–nagavanshi forest tribals? And did you serve wine every time?

—No.

The nishadin's eyes are her death sentence. Kunti refuses to lie.

—Just that one time?

—Just that one time.

—Just that one time that the vratya, the outcast, were invited?

—Yes.

—Drunk on so much wine, that nishadin mother and her five sons lay there senseless. You knew this, yet you escaped through your secret tunnel, didn't you?

—Yes, I did.

—That nishadin . . .

—Not you!

—No, my mother-in-law. I am her eldest daughter-in-law. These women with me were married to her other sons.

—But . . . you aren't widows . . .

The nishadin said with pride, We don't deny the demands of life. If we are widowed we have the right to remarry. Those who wish to can marry again. We did so. We have husbands, children.

—What will you . . . ?

—No. An eye for an eye, a tooth for a tooth, that's the way of the rajavritta. That's what Kurukshetra was all about. The lokavritta's ways are different.

—Tell me, what should I do?

—You couldn't even remember this sin. Causing six innocent forest tribals to be burnt to death to serve your own interests. That was not even a crime in your book. In our eyes, by the laws of Mother Nature, you, your sons, your allies, are all held guilty.

The nishadin came even closer. Said, See this forest? Full of resin-bearing trees? Resin is highly inflammable, do you know that?

—Yes.

—Resin oozes out of the trunks and congeals. Sometimes dry fir cones fall off the trees and roll down the hill slopes. Then, when those dry cones hit the resin, sparks fly. A fire starts. Forest fire.

—Forest fire!

—Yes. We can tell, from smelling the air, just as the other

creatures of the forest can, that a fire has started. That's why they are fleeing. Like we are.

—Where to?

—Far away, beyond the reach of the forest fire. Where there are mountains, lakes and winding rivers.

—Forest fire!

—Yes. Three blind, weak and infirm people cannot make it there. One is blind from birth, another has chosen to be blind, and you, you are the blindest of the three. You can murder innocents and then forget all about it.

—Nishadin, is it impossible to forgive me?

—To beg forgiveness is typical of the rajavritta. We don't understand such things. When the five of us came away here, others came with us. For years, this forest has looked after us.

—But the forest fire?

—The fire will do its work, then rain will quench the flames. The scorched earth will turn green again.

The nishadin fled.

Kunti sat unmoving. Her mind blank, empty of wishes, desires, thoughts and feeling.

She got up. She has to go back to the ashram. Wait for the forest fire. Dhritarashtra and Gandhari, after their loss of a hundred sons, are waiting patiently for death, waiting for the final fire to consume them.

Kunti also welcomes death. Burning alive in the flames of a forest fire, will she pray for forgiveness from a certain dead nishadin?

In the rajavritta does one beg forgiveness for killing the innocent?

Kunti does not know.

Notes

1 Nishadin: woman of the Nishad people, one of the 'uncivilized' races of ancient India chiefly living by hunting; swineherds, fishermen or fowlers by caste.

2 Hidimba: Sister of Hidimbo, the rakshasa, who bore Bhima a son named Ghatotkacha. One of Kunti's non-Aryan daughters-in-law.

3 Soon after Kunti's marriage to Pandu, one day in the forest Pandu's arrow struck a pair of mating deer—actually a sage and his wife trying for a son. The dying sage—a brahman—cursed Pandu that any attempt at sexual union with his wife would result in his death. Thus cursed, Pandu informed Kunti of his inability to sire an heir and requested her to choose another to father her child. Kunti then told him that the sage Durbasa, pleased with her service and devotion, had granted her a boon enabling her to summon any god she liked and thereafter bear his son. Pandu requested her to summon Dharma (or Yamaraj, the God of Death and Justice) and Yudhisthira was born of that union. Subsequently, according to Pandu's desire, Kunti summoned Pavana (the Wind God) who fathered Bhima and Indra (the King of the Gods, the God of Thunder), who fathered Arjuna.

4 Madri, Pandu's second wife, acquired the mantra for summoning the gods from Kunti and called upon the Ashwinikumaras (the attendant physicians of the gods) who fathered the twins Nakula and Sahadeva. One spring day, Pandu experienced a momentary lapse in his abstinence and took Madri by force. As per the curse, he died at the moment of sexual union. The widows Kunti and Madri both wished to end their lives on his pyre but finally, Madri prevailed upon Kunti to live and tend to her sons before joining Pandu in death. Kunti and the five brothers returned to Hastinapur.

5 Dhananjaya: literally, 'he who conquers settlements and lives there with all the collected wealth'; another name for Arjuna.

souvali

[While Gandhari was with child, a vaishya was in the service of Dhritarashtra. She bore a son named Yuyutsu—*Mahabharata Saranubad* by Rajsekhar Basu. Yuyutsu's mother was Souvali—*Pouranik Abidhan* by Sudhinchandra Sarkar.]

On the margins of the town live the marginalized. Their settlement is a lively, noisy place. The alleys are narrow, the houses small. Ponds here and there, surrounded by trees. Cattle sheds beside the huts. There, on the stoop of a large hut, sat Souvali. Ageing, but still not infirm. Copper skin. Salt and pepper hair braided in a long plait. Black choli. Green ghagra, yellow chunni tucked in at the waist, drawn across the breasts and thrown over one shoulder.

The woman next door said, What's this, mashi? Still waiting?

—He hasn't come yet.

—Is Souvalya coming here?

—That's what he said.

—He's been here before, hasn't he?

—He comes every now and then. Today he sat for a bit, didn't say a word . . . finally . . . why don't you carry on, dear.

—Isn't Ahana back?

—Ahana! Even her mother was dying to go. Ahana, Varunya, no one's back. They've a-l-l gone to see the mahatarpan, to watch water being offered to the spirits of the dead.

—Well, I'll be off, Ma. Still have to fetch the water.

—Carry on, dear.

Souvalya walked into the yard. The sun was setting, but it wasn't dark yet. Ashadh evenings are a long time coming. Souvalya said, Ma.

—Come, my son. Wait there, let me pour some water, wash your feet.

—No, Ma. I've had a bath already.

—Yes, you must have. Come, change into dry clothes. Rest awhile.

—May I stay the night?

—What could be better, son? Come inside.

Spacious hut. Neem-scented breeze through the window. Souvali has planted a grove of neem trees behind the house. Also an orchard of mango, jamun and other fruit trees. Sturdy green trees, guarding the hut like sentinels.

Souvalya sat on the wooden seat. Souvali bought these high, wooden lacquered stools from the nomadic traders. She brought out sweet kheer laddoos, pithas of jowar, honey. Said, Eat something, son.

—And you?

—I'll eat too. Why shouldn't I, after all?

—I did the tarpan. And you . . .

Souvali smiled, and said, You're the son. You did your duty. Today they had to grant you the first right. You are Dhritarashtra's son. If they left you out, they would have gone against dharma.

Souvalya's hair is greying. He is Souvali's son. In this house, he is Souvalya. Not Yuyutsu. At the sound of that name, his mother flares up. Yuyutsu indeed! Give the boy a name and that's the end of all responsibility!

—No, Yudhisthira was extremely careful.

—And Bhima?

—What's the point of discussing him?

—Son, did you do the tarpan for Kunti and Gandhari as well?

—No, Ma. Even if I'd tried, my tongue would have revolted.

Souvalya sighed. Said, This is the only place where I can breathe freely. But Ahana and Varunya aren't back . . . you're all alone . . .

—Not really, my dear. I have good neighbours . . . and I only have to sound the conch for people to come running . . . after the Pandava victory we . . . what happened today was such a mockery, wasn't it? Their forest exile was so long ago, their death in the forest fire, and now, after so many many days, this so-called mahatarpan! Wait and see, Yudhisthira will gather their remains and cast them in the river. Ahana and Varunya have gone to see the fun and games.

—Never went near him, never called him 'father', and today I did the tarpan for him.

—Or else his soul would not have gained release. Dasiputra! Slavechild! It's because of this dasiputra that you got water from a son's hand! Kunti! Gandhari! Gandhari never once, in all these years, acknowledged you as a Kaurava. Why should she? Just a dasiputra, after all.

Souvalya smiled slightly.

—I told them, I'll do the tarpan for my father. Not for Kunti, not for Gandhari. They never accepted me.

—Oh son, I am content.

—They exchanged glances. Finally Yudhishtira said in a dry tone, Son of Dhritarashtra! I know you are a man of conscience, son of a good woman . . .

—Can't even remember him.

—Ma! The oldest Pandava has always been different from the other brothers. He said, Do as you think right. I . . . I did the tarpan just for my father. If I hadn't, they wouldn't have been able to begin the rites. Then I came away.

—You did the right thing. And what after all would have happened had you not done so? Anyway, you did your duty.

—And you . . .

—I have no such duty, my son. Born into a vaishya family. They took us to serve as dasis from our very childhood. Then, when Gandhari was carrying, I got pregnant with you. When you were born, I forgot all my sorrows! Why does Vidura get so much respect, son? He's a dasiputra too, like you.

—Let it go, Ma! You left me too, didn't you?

—I stayed as long as they let you be with me. In the rajavritta, male offspring aren't left with their mothers for long. They are suckled by wet nurses, they stay with the dasis. I showered you with care and love, kept you safe.

—Why did you leave, Ma?

—Because they sent you off to the gurugriha, to the home of your teacher, when you were barely five. How I cried and wept, Souvalya! But even little boys aren't allowed to stay in the royal women's quarters.

Souvalya spoke softly. I used to cry too. Look all over for you. Dasiputras were sent to a separate gurugriha. Then, when the time came for training in arms, for some reason I was transferred to the same gurugriha as the Kauravas.

—What? Souvalya, you did your arms training . . .

—Who else would retrieve their arrows? Who else would fetch the birds they shot down?

—That's when I asked Gandhari to release me from my dasi status. She didn't say anything. Then, in desperation I told the head dasi, Dhruva, I'm going to live on the outskirts of town. If my son looks for me, please tell him where I am.

—And you came away?

—What else? The dasis of those days must be old now, helpless, who knows where they're lying around still, somewhere in the inner quarters of the royal household. I didn't wait for anyone. Couldn't even inform your father. He was well protected, guarded by the watchful eyes of Gandhari. If I could have I would have told him, you took my youth, you took my son, he is your flesh and blood but you never treated him so. You can stay here with your Duryodhana, I'm off.

—I've never known a father's love.

—Duryodhana meant everything to him. He used to ask Dhruva about you on the quiet. That too, just once or twice. But Souvalya, my son! I never stopped thinking about you.

On the outskirts of the town, everyone knew who Souvali was. Dhruva's brother Divya helped her a lot at the time. As the mother of a Kaurava, Souvali faced no trouble. A hut was built, readied to be lived in. Ahana and Varunya's grandmother volunteered to live with her as her dasi, saying, If you say no, where will I go? So a hut was built for her too.

—I never thought I'd find you again.

—But you did.

Souvalya nursed a secret grief, his mother had forgotten about him. But when he saw how carefully his childhood toys, tiny bangles, golden comb had been preserved all these years, it hadn't been hard at all to turn to her and call her 'Ma'.

Souvali said, So many offers of marriage! You're so beautiful, come with us, we'll take you to Dasharna, the wandering traders would tell me. But Dasharna was so far away! If I went off, there would be no news . . . and son, I waited . . . for Divya to come, to bring news of you. Ahana's grandmother and her young daughter were here, my restless mind got some comfort from them, and then . . . but you know all about it . . .

—I am at peace knowing they're with you . . .

—Why don't you change into dry clothes?

—No need, my clothes are dry now. Come, let's sit and talk awhile.

Souvali carried a lamp outside. Said, When Ahana and the others come back, they'll go straight to bed.

—You're all alone at night . . . is it safe?

—Not even a thief will dare enter this hut. No one will touch me. Everyone respects the mother of a warrior.

—No wonder I sided with the Pandavas in battle. The Kauravas called me Dasiputra, treated me like one. I detested them.

Souvali stroked her son's forehead.

—When Yudhisthira said, let those who wish to join us come, we will receive them with honour, I crossed over with no hesitation.

—What a hubbub in the town! Yuyutsu—how I dislike taking that name!—has joined the Pandavas!

—And Duryodhana said with contempt, I knew he'd join them. Ma, no one knew which side would win, which side would lose, but I knew that if I died fighting, I'd die in peace. Can you understand why I joined them?

Souvali's once-lovely lip curled in contempt. She said, All those years of constantly being ignored, all that humiliation.

—Yes, Ma. It didn't really matter to the Kauravas whether I was there or not. The humiliation . . . but I used to worry about how you might feel . . .

—I felt at peace . . .

—And after the battle . . . on the cremation ground . . . truth-fully, ma, no matter what kind of man he was . . . the savagery with which Duryodhana was killed!

—It was war, my child. There was savagery on both sides. Think of Bhima!

—And at the end . . . Bhima was so insulting to father . . . war robs man of humanity. How boastful the victors were! How arro-gantly they behaved!

—Yes, I know, my son. Now go to sleep.

—One night with you.

—I'm going to hold you close, my son. You've been lost to me since childhood.

—They knew I used to come here. They'd taunt me. Say that only dasiputras suffered such unmanly needs, cried for their mothers.

—It's true. It's in the janavritta, amongst the common people, that we are in touch with our natural emotions. Tenderness, caring, compassion, romance, love, anger, jealousy. But in the rajavritta, you know how they keep such natural emotions strictly in check.

—Yes, you're right.

—And that's their downfall. It's always been power, greed, arro-gance and enmity that's caused the ruin of the rajavritta.

—It's so nice to talk to you like this, ma.

—You'll leave at dawn?

—Yes, Ma. Yudhisthira told me, O Son of Dhritarashtra . . . go and tell your mother . . . the tarpan was performed properly. She may not know . . .

Souvalya fell asleep. Souvali lifted his arm onto the bed.

Arranged the pillow more comfortably under his head. How grey his hair was, how lined his forehead! All those years of humiliation, disrespect and unkindness had caused these furrows to appear.

A soft knock on the door. Must be Ahana. Come to sleep with her.

Opening the door a crack, Souvali whispered, Not tonight, Ahana. Souvalya's sleeping here.

—Granny! Ma asked if you . . .

Souvali went out and shut the door. Said, Go fetch your mother, dear.

Ahana's mother came. Asked, Is there anything you need me to do for you before I go to bed?

—Like what?

—Any death rite related stuff? After all, your son did the tarpan . . .

—Go to bed, Chandra. What death rites? Who was Dhritarashtra to me?

—What do you mean? He was your . . .

—Son's father. And my son has done his duty.

—But . . .

—I'm just a dasi. Was I his wedded wife, that I should undergo the death rites? In the royal household, so many of us dasis come and go, so many bear children. . . observe ashaucha, the contamination rites? Do tarpan? Wear white cloth, fast? Why?

Souvali's eyes are gleaming. She says, I'll feast on sweet kheer laddoos, ghee-rich jowar pithas, golden honey. And after I'm full, I'll sleep peacefully holding my son in my arms.

Souvali shut the door. It feels good to have defied the dead Dhritarashtra. In the royal household, the other dasis would be roaming around in white widows' clothing, eating only the prescribed meagre fare.

Will Souvali go to hell for this?

Or to heaven?

Souvali tells herself, Why worry about all that? I'm hungry, so I'll eat. I left that place of my own free will. Today too I'll let my own dharma tell me what's right.

Happily, Souvali washed her face and hands. It is said that Krishna Dwaipayan Vyas is going to write about this righteous war . . .

So let him! Souvali doesn't want even a mention of her name anywhere.

Her son is foolish. Following the norms and customs of royalty even though he's one of the common folk.

She thinks to herself, If you must learn, learn from your mother. I was nothing but a dasi in the royal household but here, amongst the common people, I'm a free woman.

And she begins to eat. Food cooked by her has never tasted so good. When will Souvalya realize? That even the Pandavas will never accept him as one of their own?